Jesus
was a Refugee

Andrew McDonough

Father Abraham

King David

Dad

Mum

Me

My name is Jesus, son of Joseph, son of David, son of Abraham. This is my family.

This is Bethlehem where I was born.

Bethlehem was my home. Now it is not my home.

We can visit, but it is not safe to stay for too long. Not while the son of BAD King Herod sits on the throne.

When we visit Bethlehem I play with the girls.

There are no boys my age in Bethlehem.

The women in Bethlehem are sad.
My aunties cry a lot when they see me.

My name is Joseph, son of Jacob, son of David, son of Abraham. This is my wife Mary and our son Jesus.
I am a refugee.

Let me tell you our story . . .

When our son was small, wise men came. They said our son would be king. They gave him gifts of gold, frankincense and precious myrrh.

One night, an angel spoke to me in a dream. "Get up! Grab your son, go to Egypt! King Herod is looking for your boy. He wants to kill him!"

We fled.

We hid . . .

We walked and we walked . . .

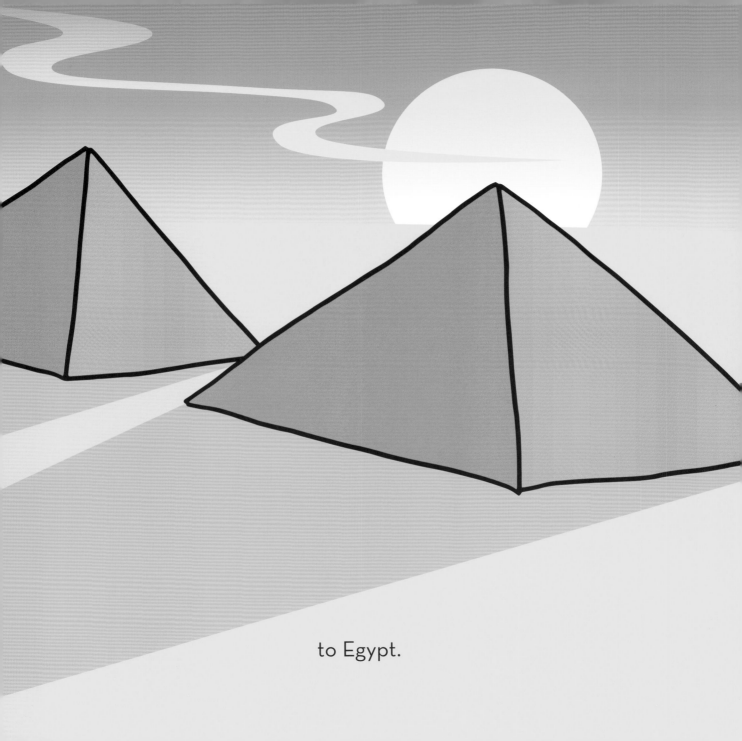

to Egypt.

Welcome to Border Security Mr Joseph. So, you wish to enter Egypt? If we can just review your documents.

It says here that you are Joseph son of Jacob. But it says here you are Joseph son of Heli. What is your father's name? Tell me, who are you Mr Joseph?

You say you're from Bethlehem, but it says here you're from Nazareth. Where do you really come from Mr Joseph?

Did you say this woman is your wife and this boy is your son? But the dates on these two certificates are a little irregular. Is this really your family Mr Joseph?

Gold, frankincense and precious myrrh! I'll look after these for you. Welcome to Egypt Mr Joseph.

Then one night, the angel returned and spoke to me in a dream. "Get up! Grab your son, go back to Israel! King Herod is dead."

We left Egypt.

We walked . . .

and we walked . . .

to Bethlehem. But it still wasn't safe to stay in Bethlehem.
So we walked and walked to Nazareth in Galilee.

Nazareth is now our home.

My name is Joseph, this is my
wife Mary and our son Jesus.

Do not forget, never forget,
Jesus was a refugee.

The Back Page

Jesus was a Refugee is based on that unsettling bit of the Christmas story in Matthew 2:1-23. This never makes it into the end of year nativity play. Fair enough. Who wants to traumatise the kids with Bad King Herod, the atrocities in Bethlehem and a dull ending where the family drifts off to Nazareth. Compare that to the five star, family friendly version where the bad guy's an inn keeper, the crisis a travel accommodation mix up, and it all ends with a magnificent shepherd dancing, angel singing, expensive gifting, new born baby finale. So, why tell the escape to Egypt story to children? Simply because it is a Jesus story and it mirrors the story of 70 million people including 25 million children around the world who have been forced from their homes.

Over the last 27 years I have worked with hundreds of refugees. This story is for Hoa who arrived in Australia as a disabled orphan, then returned to Vietnam to found a community run entirely by people with disabilities. It's for David Jock, who as a child separated from his parents walked from Sudan to Ethiopia and now mentors young people from all cultures. It's for my children, who snuggled up to mums who had lost babies and played with kids who didn't share their language. And this story is for your children. May they know safety from danger and grow up to treat any refugee they meet as if they were Jesus.

Before the story

You might like to do some drawings together.

Read the story

After the story

You may both have lots of questions. If you're after refugee facts and figures, visit the UN Refugee Agency website. If you're wondering why there were no boys in Bethlehem, read Matthew 2:16-18. If you're wondering what prompted the Border Security guard's questions, compare the family trees in Matthew 1:16 and Luke 3:23. The 'Where do you come from?' question was prompted by comparing Luke 2:39 with Matthew 2:16. If the Border Security guard read Matthew 1:18-25, he would understand the 'irregularities' between Jesus' birth certificate and his parent's marriage certificate.

God's blessing,
Andrew

Matthew 2:1–23 (CEV)

When Jesus was born in the village of Bethlehem in Judea, Herod was king. During this time some wise men from the east came to Jerusalem and said, "Where is the child born to be king of the Jews? We saw his star in the east and have come to worship him." When King Herod heard about this, he was worried, and so was everyone else in Jerusalem. Herod brought together the chief priests and the teachers of the Law of Moses and asked them, "Where will the Messiah be born?" They told him, "He will be born in Bethlehem, just as the prophet wrote, 'Bethlehem in the land of Judea, you are very important among the towns of Judea. From your town will come a leader, who will be like a shepherd for my people Israel.'" Herod secretly called in the wise men and asked them when they had first seen the star. He told them, "Go to Bethlehem and search carefully for the child. As soon as you find him, let me know. I want to go and worship him too." The wise men listened to what the king said and then left. And the star they had seen in the east went on ahead of them until it stopped over the place where the child was. They were thrilled and excited to see the star. When the men went into the house and saw the child with Mary, his mother, they knelt down and worshipped him. They took out their gifts of gold, frankincense, and myrrh and gave them to him. Later they were warned in a dream not to return to Herod, and they went back home by another road. After the wise men had gone, an angel from the Lord appeared to Joseph in a dream and said, "Get up! Hurry and take the child and his mother to Egypt! Stay there until I tell you to return, because Herod is looking for the child and wants to kill him."

That night, Joseph got up and took his wife and the child to Egypt, where they stayed until Herod died. So the Lord's promise came true, just as the prophet had said, "I called my son out of Egypt." When Herod found out that the wise men from the east had tricked him, he was very angry. He gave orders for his men to kill all the boys who lived in or near Bethlehem and were two years old and younger. This was based on what he had learned from the wise men. So the Lord's promise came true, just as the prophet Jeremiah had said, "In Ramah a voice was heard crying and weeping loudly. Rachel was mourning for her children, and she refused to be comforted, because they were dead."

After King Herod died, an angel from the Lord appeared in a dream to Joseph while he was still in Egypt. The angel said, "Get up and take the child and his mother back to Israel. The people who wanted to kill him are now dead." Joseph got up and left with them for Israel. But when he heard that Herod's son Archelaus was now ruler of Judea, he was afraid to go there. Then in a dream he was told to go to Galilee, and they went to live there in the town of Nazareth. So the Lord's promise came true, just as the prophet had said, "He will be called a Nazarene."

Published edition © 2018 Lost Sheep Resources Pty Ltd
Text and illustrations © 2018 Andrew McDonough

© 2018 Lost Sheep Resources Pty Ltd. Lost Sheep is a trademark of Lost Sheep Resources Pty Ltd.

This edition published 2018 Sarah Grace Publishing an imprint of Malcolm Down Publishing Ltd
ISBN 9781912863013
sarahgracepublishing.co.uk

All rights reserved. No part of this book may be reproduced in any form or by any means without prior permission from the publishers. If you wish to use this story in a group setting, you can purchase and download the images from our store at lostsheep.com.au. Do not scan the book onto your computer.

The Bible text is from The Bible for Today (Contemporary English Version) © American Bible Society 1991, 1995. Used by permission of the Bible Society in Australia Inc (1995), GPO Box 507, Canberra ACT 2601.

First printing July 2018
27 26 25 24 23 22 21 20 19 18   10 9 8 7 6 5 4 3 2 1

British Library Cataloguing-in-Publication data
A catalogue record for this book is available from the British Library

Gold smuggler: Hoa Van Stone
Desert guide: David Jock
Crayons supplier: David McDonough

Please place this book in a clear sealed plastic bag before passing through border security.

Designed and published by Lost Sheep

Lost Sheep, PO Box 3191, Unley SA 5061, Australia
info@lostsheep.com.au
lostsheep.com.au

Printed in the United Kingdom